THIS CANDLEWICK BOOK BELONGS TO:

_____

_____

_____

_____

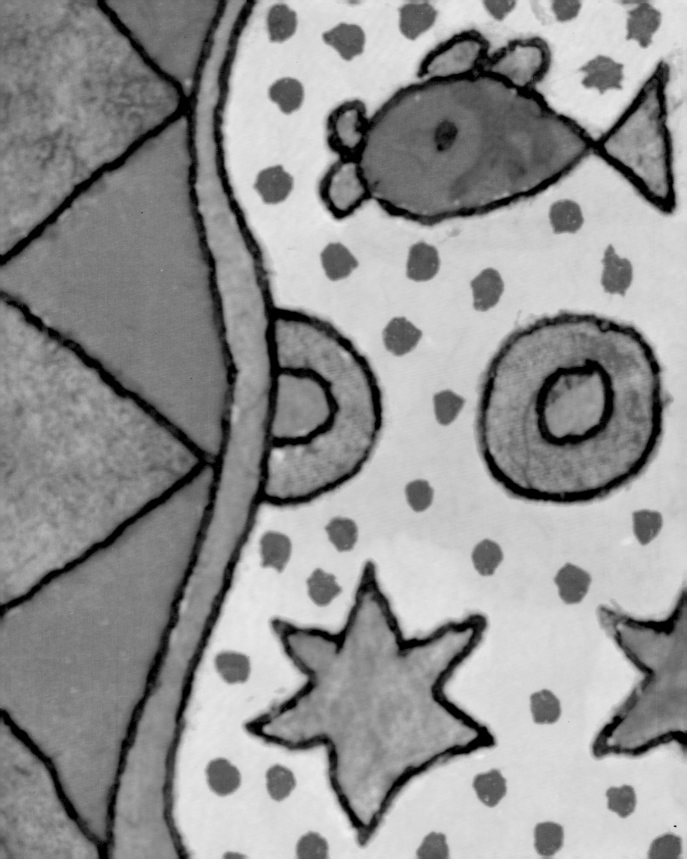

FOR PEPPER & COLIN.

Copyright © 1990 by Marcia Williams
First U.S. paperback edition 1994
First published in Great Britain in 1990 by Walker Books Ltd., London.
Library of Congress Cataloging-in-Publication Data
Williams, Marcia.
Joseph and his magnificent coat of many colors / by Marcia Williams.
—1st U.S. ed.
Originally published: London: Walker Books, 1990.
Summary: Retells the Bible story in which Joseph's jealous brothers
sell him into slavery in Egypt, where due to his ability to interpret
dreams, he is made governor of the country.
ISBN 1-56402-019-3 (hardcover)
1. Joseph (Son of Jacob)—Juvenile literature.
2. Bible stories, English—O.T. Genesis.
[1. Joseph (Son of Jacob)   2. Bible stories—O.T.]   I. Title.
BS580.J6W58   1992   222'.1109505—dc20   91-71843
ISBN 1-56402-265-X (paperback)
10 9 8 7 6 5 4 3 2 1
Printed in Hong Kong
The pictures for this book were done in watercolor and pen and ink.
Candlewick Press
2067 Massachusetts Avenue, Cambridge, Massachusetts 02140

JOSEPH
and his
MAGNIFICENT COAT
OF MANY COLORS

by
Marcia Williams

CANDLEWICK PRESS
CAMBRIDGE, MASSACHUSETTS

There once lived, in the land of Canaan,

a farmer called Jacob.

Jacob had twelve fine sons,

but the one he loved best was Joseph.

HAPPY 17th BIRTHDAY

Jacob gave Joseph a magnificent coat of many colors,

In Joseph's first dream,

he and his brothers were binding corn.

In this dream, Joseph's sheaf rose and stood upright,

and his brothers' sheaves bowed down before it.

In Joseph's second dream,

the sun, the moon, and eleven stars

bowed down before him as though he were king.

Joseph's father believed the dreams meant

that Joseph would become a great ruler.

"Let's kill the dreamer," they said to each other.

"We can pretend that a ferocious animal ate him.

Then our father will pay some attention to us."

But one of the brothers, named Reuben,

persuaded the others not to kill Joseph.

Instead, they stripped off his magnificent coat

and cast him into a pit.

Then, at midday, as the brothers sat down to eat,

they saw a company of Ishmaelites ride over the hill,

their camels loaded with spices to sell in Egypt.

Help!

The brothers decided to sell Joseph to the travelers

in exchange for a bag of silver.

Then they dipped Joseph's beautiful coat in blood

and returned home to their father.

Jacob was heartbroken when he saw the coat.

Believing that Joseph had been killed by wild beasts,

he put on sackcloth and mourned his favorite son.

Now it so happened that one morning Pharaoh

sat puzzling over two strange dreams.

His wise man could not fathom their meaning,

so Joseph was brought out of prison

and asked to interpret them.

The seven years of plenty passed.

Then a terrible famine swept across Egypt.

Joseph opened the storehouses.

People came from far and wide to buy grain,

for the famine had descended on many lands.

The brothers pleaded with Joseph to enslave them instead, and set Benjamin free.

Joseph saw then that his brothers had changed.

He knew that they loved Benjamin and their father

and would give their lives for them.

MARCIA WILLIAMS's distinctive style developed through the illustrated letters she sent from boarding school to her parents overseas. It was motherhood, though, and a period spent later as a nursery school teacher that inspired her to produce books for children. She is the author-illustrator of several picture books, including other stories from the Bible, a retelling of *Don Quixote*, and *Greek Myths for Young Children*, all written with the intention of making them accessible and amusing to children.